SADIQ
and the
Pet Problem

BY SIMAN NUURALI

ART BY ANJAN SARKAR

PICTURE WINDOW BOOKS
a capstone imprint

Sadiq is published by Picture Window Books,
a Capstone imprint
1710 Roe Crest Drive
North Mankato, Minnesota 56003
www.mycapstone.com

Library of Congress Cataloging-in-Publication Data
Names: Nuurali, Siman, author. | Sarkar, Anjan, illustrator.
Title: Sadiq and the pet problem / by Siman Nuurali ; illustrated by Anjan
    Sarkar.
Description: North Mankato, Minnesota : Picture Window Books, [2019] |
    Series: Sadiq | Summary: Sadiq's third-grade class decides that they want
    a classroom pet, and their teacher, Ms. Battersby, is OK with the idea, so
    the students form a club to decide what kind of pet to get, and to
    research how to take care of it.
Identifiers: LCCN 2018050218| ISBN 9781515838807 (hardcover) | ISBN
    9781515845683 (pbk.) | ISBN 9781515838845 (ebook pdf)
Subjects: LCSH: Pets—Juvenile fiction. | Elementary schools—Juvenile
    fiction. | Muslim families—United States—Juvenile fiction. | Children of
    immigrants—Juvenile fiction. | Africans—United States—Juvenile fiction.
    | CYAC: Pets—Fiction. | Schools—Fiction. | Muslims—United
    States—Fiction. | Immigrants—Fiction. | Africans—United States—
Fiction.
Classification: LCC PZ7.1.N9 Sap 2019 | DDC [Fic]—dc23
LC record available at https://lccn.loc.gov/2018050218

Design Element: Shutterstock/Irtsya
Designer: Brann Garvey

Printed and bound in China.
1671

TABLE OF CONTENTS

FACTS ABOUT SOMALIA

- Most Somali people belong to one of four major groups: the Darod, Isaaq, Hawiye, and Dir.
- Many Somalis are nomadic. That means they travel from place to place. They search for water, food, and land for their animals.
- Somalia is mostly desert. It doesn't rain often there.
- The camel is an important animal to Somali people. Camels can survive a long time without food or water.
- Around ninety-nine percent of all Somalis are Muslim.

SOMALI TERMS

awoowe (ah-WOH-weh)—grandfather

ayeyo (ah-YEY-yoh)—grandmother

baba (BAH-baah)—a common word for father

hooyo (HOY-yoh)—mother

qalbi (KUHL-bee)—my heart

salaam (sa-LAHM)—a short form of Arabic greeting, used by many Muslims. It also means "peace."

wiilkeyga (wil-KAY-gaah)—my son

CHAPTER 1

A BUNNY AT SCHOOL!

When Sadiq walked past Ms. Colt's classroom, a crowd of kids was standing by her desk. They were playing with a bunny.

Sadiq walked into his classroom. "Did you see the bunny?" he asked his friends Zaza and Manny.

"Huh?" said Zaza, confused.

"Are you daydreaming again?" asked Manny, laughing.

"No," Sadiq answered. "Ms. Colt's class has a bunny! It had fluffy white fur. The kids looked really happy to be playing with it. I think it must have been their class pet!"

Abs and Maryam walked into the classroom.

"Hi, Abs! Hi, Maryam!" said Zaza. "Guess what? Sadiq saw a bunny in Ms. Colt's class."

"Cool!" said Maryam. "I didn't know we could have class pets."

"I don't know if we can have one. I don't think I have ever seen one in any other class," said Sadiq. He felt sad.

"We could ask Ms. Battersby," said Abs.

That gave Sadiq an idea. "We could have a pet club!" he said. "We can come up with ideas for a class pet and research them."

"Yes!" Maryam said. "We could talk to the rest of the class and see what they think."

"But first we have to ask Ms. Battersby," said Manny.

Their teacher came into the room.

"Hi, Ms. Battersby!" Sadiq said.

"Hello, children!" said Ms. Battersby. "You look excited."

"We wanted to ask if we can have a class pet," said Sadiq.

"And a pet club," added Manny. "The Pet Club will help our class find a pet."

Ms. Battersby looked surprised. Then she smiled. "You must have noticed Ms. Colt's new rabbit," she said. "Pets are a lot of hard work. Can I count on the Pet Club to help assign classmates to feed, clean, and play with our class pet?"

Sadiq and his friends nodded.

"Okay then!" Ms. Battersby said. "We can get a class pet."

The group cheered.

"We could get a bunny or a hamster or a turtle!" Maryam suggested.

"What should we name it?" Manny asked.

Abs smiled. "I think Rocky would be a cool name for a turtle!"

"Slow down, kids," said Ms. Battersby, laughing. "We haven't even decided what kind of pet to get!"

"How will we ever choose?" Sadiq asked.

"Maybe we can do a survey. We can talk with our whole class and see what everyone likes," said Ms. Battersby.

Sadiq and his friends high-fived.

* * *

Sadiq walked home from school later that day with Zaza and his sister Aliya.

"Did you see that Ms. Colt's class has a new bunny?" Sadiq asked Aliya.

"No!" Aliya said. "Not fair! How come my class doesn't have a pet?"

"Ours doesn't have one either," said Zaza, shrugging.

"But we started a Pet Club," Sadiq said. "Ms. Battersby said that we can get a pet. We just have to help figure out what kind of pet would be best for our class."

"I've been bugging Hooyo and Baba to get us a pet for years," said Aliya sadly.

"You have?" asked Sadiq.

Aliya nodded. "They say we can't have one because Rania is allergic to a lot of things. But maybe I can convince Mr. Dawes to get a class pet. What kind of pet are you thinking?"

"I don't know," Sadiq said. "Maybe a turtle?"

"Turtles are so boring!" said Aliya.

"Well, what do you suggest?" Zaza asked.

"I've always wanted a rat," said Aliya. "They're so cute!"

"Eww, rats aren't cute!" Sadiq said. "They're gross!"

"*You're* gross!" Aliya playfully bumped shoulders with him as they walked toward their house.

CHAPTER 2

BRAINSTORMING PETS

The next day, Ms. Battersby stood patiently at the front of the room while the class settled down.

"Good morning, children," she said after everyone was seated. "Some of your classmates have come to me with an idea. They have started the Pet Club. They are hoping they can help our class adopt a pet."

Laughter and chatter broke out.

"Well, it seems like we're all on board!" Ms. Battersby said, laughing. "Remember, caring for pets is a lot of hard work. Everyone will have to help out." She paused and picked up a dry-erase marker. "Let's share some ideas for class pets."

"What if we got a rat?" Ellie said. "They're really smart and playful."

"Good idea, Ellie," Ms. Battersby said. She wrote it on the board.

"My family keeps chickens at home," said Avina. "Maybe our class can adopt one."

"Chickens are a lot of work. I'm not sure that they would make a good classroom pet," said Ms. Battersby.

"How about a scorpion?" said Kianna.

"Scorpions sting sometimes," the teacher replied. "We need to make sure the pet is safe around children."

"Let's get a cat!" Dale called out.

"I love cats, but lots of people are allergic to them," Ms. Battersby said. "Unfortunately we can't have one as a classroom pet. What other ideas do you have?"

"Parakeets are nice," said Abs. "We had one when I was little. They sing a lot and sometimes sit on your head!"

Ms. Battersby smiled and wrote it down. "Anyone else have an idea?" she asked.

"I like tarantulas!" said Maryam.

"Goldfish are colorful and pretty," said Odin.

"A snake! They can be fun to watch," said Zaza.

Ms. Battersby wrote those three ideas down as well. "This is a great list," she said.

The list read:

- rat
- parakeet
- tarantula
- goldfish
- snake

"How do you think we should decide what pet is best for our class?" Ms. Battersby asked.

Several hands went up. Ms. Battersby pointed to Abs.

"The Pet Club could research all the animals on our list. That way we can pick the one that would be the best class pet."

"Great thought, Abs. What do the rest of you think, Pet Club?" Ms. Battersby asked.

"That's a great idea," said Sadiq. "Could we use our library time to do research?"

"Certainly!" said Ms. Battersby. "We have library time this afternoon."

* * *

Later that day during library time, the members of the Pet Club each found a book on one of the pets. They sat around the table and began to read.

After about twenty minutes of researching, it was clear the list they had would not work.

"A snake could grow to be too big for us to keep, and it might bite someone," said Maryam.

"It says here that parakeets can get loud," said Manny, shaking his head in frustration.

"I don't know if there is much we could learn from keeping a goldfish. They also don't live very long," Abs said.

"Tarantulas need lots of care. They can eat up to six crickets a week! Plus lots of people are afraid of spiders," said Zaza.

"Rats can be really smelly, and they need a lot of space," said Sadiq, closing his book.

The Pet Club members were disappointed.

"I don't know how we will ever find a class pet," said Maryam sadly.

"What if we talk to our families and friends about any pets they've had? It might help us come up with some new ideas," said Sadiq.

"That's a great idea, Sadiq!" said Abs. "Let's all meet tomorrow and share what we find out!"

The five friends all nodded in agreement. Soon the bell rang, and everyone headed back to class.

CHAPTER 3

WILDLIFE WONDER

That night Sadiq watched as his mother braided Amina's hair. She had already finished Rania's.

"Did you have pets growing up in Somalia, Hooyo?" he asked.

His mother shook her head as she worked her fingers through Amina's hair. "I didn't, *qalbi.* We owned a lot of cattle, but those were not pets. The herdsmen who worked for my baba would take the cattle grazing outside."

"How far away, Hooyo?" Sadiq asked. "As far as our school?"

"Farther than that, *wiilkeyga!*" she said. "They would move the cattle hundreds of miles until they found enough water and pasture."

"Were you sad your family didn't have any pets?" Sadiq asked.

"Not really," his mother said. "Your *ayeyo* would put out milk for the neighborhood cats. And we had plenty of animals around! Unlike pets, our animals provided us with meat, milk, and butter. Sometimes when we needed money, your *awoowe* would sell one or two of the cows or bulls, even though he didn't like to do that."

That made Sadiq think. The animals Hooyo had growing up weren't pets at all. That wasn't very helpful for choosing a school pet. But it was interesting to think about.

After dinner, Sadiq went outside to play. Maryam, Zaza, and Abs were there too.

"What did you learn about pets?" Sadiq asked them.

"When my baba was a kid he lived far outside the city. He didn't have pets, but at night he could hear lions!" said Maryam.

"My stepsister is afraid of snakes," said Abs, giggling. "She couldn't stand talking about them. It was so funny!"

"My mom didn't have pets either," Zaza said. "But our neighbor, Ms. Olive, works at a wildlife center. My mom said she could bring us there tomorrow after school."

"That would be really fun!" Sadiq said. "We can invite Manny too."

* * *

The next afternoon, the Pet Club members all got permission to go to the wildlife center. Zaza's mom, Faiza, walked with them.

"You guys are going to love this place!" Zaza said as they walked. "They have tons of different animals."

"I hope this will give us some new ideas," said Sadiq.

"Me too," said Maryam. "None of the pets we researched seem like good choices. Except for maybe the goldfish."

"Have you thought about a guinea pig?" Faiza asked. "Zaza's brother has one as a class pet."

"Good idea!" said Sadiq.

"I love guinea pigs!" Abs said.

"Me too!" said Manny. "I'll do some research on them tonight."

* * *

When they arrived at the wildlife center, Sadiq was surprised at how many animals there were. Snakes, tortoises, lizards, and even a peacock! Every few minutes, the peacock opened its tail into a giant fan!

In another pen was a one-eyed llama. It kept moving its head in different directions to look at everyone.

In one cage, Sadiq spotted a lizard. He walked over to get a closer look. "You guys! Come see this!" he shouted.

The rest of the crew ran over. They read the label: *Bearded Dragon.*

"Do you know why it's called a bearded dragon?" a woman asked. Her name tag said *Ms. Olive.*

"Is it because of its neck?" asked Abs.

"That's exactly why! They puff out their necks when they are excited or angry," said Ms. Olive. "Some people think it looks like a beard."

"Is it easy to care for?" asked Maryam.

"Yes!" said Ms. Olive. "They just need some grass, rocks, and sticks in their box. They don't like to be cold, so they should be near a window with lots of sunshine. They also like to have ultraviolet lights for warmth. They don't eat a lot. And they can live for many years. They make great pets!"

"But why is it in the wildlife center?" Manny asked. "Isn't this where animals go who are hurt?"

"Yes, this is a rehabilitation center. That means we help animals heal after they are sick or injured," Ms. Olive explained. "This lizard was found out in the wild. But bearded dragons are not supposed to live in the wild here in the United States. Someone must've decided they didn't want him as a pet anymore and let him go. He is in need of a loving home."

The children looked at each other.

"Are you thinking what I'm thinking?" Zaza asked.

"Yes!" said Sadiq.

CHAPTER 4

DECISION TIME

The next day at school, the Pet Club walked to the front of the class. They presented what they had learned from their research.

"We went through the list of animals our class came up with," Zaza said. "And we researched all of them."

"We can't keep a parakeet because they can be noisy," Manny said. "They could distract everyone!"

"We read about caring for a snake," Maryam said, "but some can get very big. They can also bite." She shivered a little bit.

"Rats need a lot of room and exercise," said Sadiq. "It might be hard to care for them over weekends and school breaks."

"Tarantulas can also make good pets, but they are scary to a lot of people," Abs said. "Including me!"

"We want to find a pet that everyone will be excited about," Sadiq said. "We came up with a few options."

"One is a goldfish. They don't live very long, but they're good pets and easy to take care of," Zaza said.

"Another is a guinea pig," said Manny. "They like people, but you have to be gentle with them. And we would need to make sure it has a lot of things to chew on! There is one up for adoption at the animal rescue."

"The last one is a kind of lizard called a bearded dragon. The Pet Club went to see one at the wildlife center," said Sadiq.

"They are easy to care for," Maryam added. "If they have a good home, they can live a very long time."

"We're going to have a vote. This time it's between three pets: a goldfish, a guinea pig, and a bearded dragon," said Zaza.

Zaza and Maryam handed out index cards.

"Everyone should write down their first choice for a pet," explained Abs.

Once everyone had an index card, the members of the Pet Club also sat down at their desks to vote.

In a few minutes, everyone was done.

Sadiq went around the class and collected the cards. He handed them to Ms. Battersby to add up all the votes. She sorted through the cards and put them into three different piles as she counted.

The class could hardly wait to hear the results. The children were whispering to their neighbors and guessing which pet would win.

Then Ms. Battersby stood in front of the class. "The results are in!" she announced. "There are eight votes for the guinea pig. Three votes are for the goldfish. The remaining ten votes are for the bearded dragon, so that will be our class pet!"

There were a couple of groans from the class, but most of the kids were excited.

"We will go pick him up this weekend!" Zaza said. "My mom said she can drive us on Sunday."

"Perfect," said Ms. Battersby. "I will buy some supplies this weekend. We'll welcome him into our classroom first thing on Monday morning!"

"We should call him Lenny!" someone shouted from the back of the class. "Lenny the Lizard."

Everyone laughed.

CHAPTER 5

PET PICKUP

On Sunday morning, Sadiq woke up bright and early. He was very excited!

Today Zaza's mom was going to take the Pet Club to the wildlife center so they could adopt Lenny the Lizard!

By the time Sadiq got downstairs, his family was already eating breakfast.

"Salaam!" Sadiq said.

"Salaam, wiilkeyga," said Baba, smiling. "Hooyo tells me your class pet has been chosen."

"Yes, Baba!" said Sadiq. "Zaza's mom is taking us to pick up Lenny the Lizard today. He's a bearded dragon."

"What do they eat?" Nuurali asked.

"Ms. Olive said he needs to eat crickets or mealworms every other day," Sadiq said. "He also likes vegetables like shredded carrots and lettuce."

"What kind of container will he live in?" Aliya asked.

"He needs a big container," Sadiq said. He poured himself a bowl of cereal. "And lots of rocks, dirt, and sticks. He likes to have a place to hide too. We'll keep his box on a window with plenty of sun. We also need to get ultraviolet lamps to give him more heat and light."

"Will you get to bring him home sometimes?" Aliya asked.

"Maybe," Sadiq said. "Someone will have to take care of him over the school breaks. Did you ever ask Mr. Dawes about a class pet?"

Aliya nodded. "He said that we can get one, but first we need to come up with a schedule of chores and who will take care of the pet."

"Cool!" Sadiq said. He quickly ate his breakfast and was putting on his shoes when he heard the doorbell ring.

He ran toward the front door and opened it. Zaza, Manny, Maryam, and Abs were all standing at the door, grinning.

They piled into Faiza's car and were on their way!

As soon as Faiza parked at the wildlife center, the Pet Club members hurried out of the car and went inside. They found Ms. Olive sitting at her desk. She looked up and smiled brightly when she saw her visitors.

"I see you couldn't stay away," said Ms. Olive. She winked at Sadiq and his friends.

Zaza spoke up. "We are here to adopt Lenny the Lizard!"

"Lenny? Oh, do you mean the bearded dragon you were looking at when you came here yesterday?" Ms. Olive asked.

"Yes," replied Sadiq. "We voted yesterday, and everyone agreed that he would make a good class pet."

"Oh, I am so sorry," said Ms. Olive. "I didn't know you were interested in adopting him. I thought you were just curious. A little boy came in with his father this morning and adopted him!"

It was silent for a few moments while they all took in the sad news.

"That's okay, Ms. Olive," said Sadiq quietly.

"We should have told you yesterday we wanted him. We didn't know if the whole class would agree to have him," Abs said.

"Thank you for your help," said Zaza.

The kids quietly left the center, feeling discouraged.

CHAPTER 6

A NEW PET

After a silent car ride back to Zaza's, the Pet Club gathered in a park nearby. Sadiq, Maryam, and Zaza sat on the swings and swung slowly and quietly. Abs and Manny sat on a bench nearby. No one was sure what to do next.

Manny broke the silence. "I know we all really wanted Lenny," he said. "But the guinea pig got almost as many votes as Lenny. And I found one available at an animal rescue nearby."

They all perked up.

"Her name is Muffin," Manny said. "And she looks cuddly and playful."

"I love that name," said Abs.

"Guinea pigs are so cute!" said Zaza.

"Could we go get it today?" Sadiq asked.

"Let's go ask my mom!" Zaza said.

Without another word, the kids all sprinted back to Zaza's house.

* * *

Faiza agreed to bring the Pet Club to the animal rescue. But first, she said, they needed to ask their teacher for permission.

Faiza sent Ms. Battersby an email explaining what was going on.

Ms. Battersby responded right away. She thought a guinea pig would make a great pet! Ms. Battersby said she would call the rescue soon to get more information.

In the meantime, the Pet Club members all piled into Faiza's car again and drove to the rescue. When they arrived, Sadiq was the first one out of the car. "Let's go, Pet Club!" he said. They followed him inside.

They walked into the lobby and could hear dogs barking, birds tweeting, and cats meowing. It was very exciting!

"Hi, I'm Ellyn," the woman behind the counter said. "Can I help you?"

"We came to ask about a guinea pig," said Sadiq.

"Oh, do you mean Muffin?" replied Ellyn. "I think your teacher, Ms. Battersby, just called about her."

Sadiq nodded. "That's right!"

"We promise to take good care of Muffin if you allow us to have her. She is going to be a class pet," said Manny.

"I think that's a great idea!" said Ellyn. "She really loves people, especially children. After talking with your teacher, it seems like she will be a great fit for your class."

"Why are you giving her away?" asked Zaza.

"Her previous owner was moving to a new apartment, where they don't allow any animals," said Ellyn sadly. She stood up. "Follow me, and I'll introduce you."

The Pet Club followed Ellyn into a back room. There were hamsters, rats, and guinea pigs in cages all around. "She should also be allowed out of her cage every day for at least fifteen minutes to get some exercise. And her cage needs to be cleaned once a week," Ellyn said.

"What do we feed her?" Abs asked.

"She likes to eat vegetables, fruit, and guinea pig food," Ellyn said. "And she needs fresh water every day."

Faiza turned to Zaza. "Should we bring her home for the night?" she asked. "Your brother can help us take care of her, since he has one as a class pet. We can get some supplies from the store on our way home."

"Yeah!" cheered Zaza.

* * *

The next morning, the Pet Club members got to school early. They met in the classroom and covered Muffin's cage with a blanket.

As their classmates walked in, there were a lot of excited whispers. Many asked if they could see Lenny. Ms. Battersby explained that the Pet Club had a surprise.

"We weren't able to adopt Lenny," Sadiq said. The class looked disappointed at first. "But we got a pretty awesome pet anyway!"

"Anyone want to take a guess what it is?" Abs asked.

"Is it a goldfish?" shouted Jeffrey.

"I bet it's a hamster!" called Kianna.

Sadiq pulled away the blanket to show Muffin sitting in her cage.

In seconds, the whole class surrounded her. They *ooh*ed and *ahh*ed over her. Some started planning all the fun games they would play with her, and the treats they would give her. Muffin was a hit with everyone!

After class had let out and the children were headed to recess, Ms. Battersby called to the members of the Pet Club to stay behind.

"That was a very lovely thing you did for our class. You're very good at this," she said. "I was thinking . . . my mom lives alone. I think a pet would be a great friend for her. Do you think your club could find a pet to keep her company?"

"Would you let us do that?" asked Abs.

"Of course!" said Ms. Battersby. "I think you could help a lot of people match up with the perfect pet for them."

"We will need to interview your mom so we can find the perfect pet for her," said Sadiq.

"That would be wonderful! I will set up a time for you all to meet," Ms. Battersby said, smiling.

Everyone cheered, and they ran out to recess.

GLOSSARY

adopt (uh-DAHPT)—to take a person or animal into your family

allergic (uh-LUR-jik)—having an allergy to something that can cause you to sneeze, develop a rash, or have some other unpleasant reaction

assign (uh-SINE)—to give someone a job to do

herdsmen (HURDS-men)—keepers of herds of livestock

interview (IN-tur-vyoo)—a meeting at which someone is asked questions

parakeet (PAR-uh-keet)—a small parrot with brightly colored feathers and a long, pointed tail

pasture (PAS-chur)—grazing land for animals

permission (pur-MISH-uhn)—an agreement to allow something to happen

previous (PREE-vee-uhs)—happening before in time or order

research (REE-surch)—to collect information about a subject through reading, investigating, or experimenting

scorpion (SKOR-pee-uhn)—an animal related to the spider with a long, jointed tail that ends in a poisonous stinger

survey (sur-VAY)—a study of the opinions or experiences of a group of people, based on their responses to questions

tarantula (tuh-RAN-chuh-luh)—a large, hairy spider found mainly in warm regions

ultraviolet light (uhl-truh-VYE-uh-lit LITE)—a type of light that is given off by the sun and cannot be seen by the human eye

wildlife (WILDE-life)—wild animals

TALK ABOUT IT

1. If you were in Sadiq's class, which pet would you have wanted to get—a guinea pig, a goldfish, or a bearded dragon? Explain why.

2. Have you ever had a pet, either at home or in class? If so, what kind of pet was it, and what did you like about it? If not, what kind of pet would you most want to have?

3. Talk about some of the responsibilities involved in owning a pet. What do you need to do to take care of it?

WRITE IT DOWN

1. Pretend you are in Sadiq's class and write a letter to the previous owner of Muffin. Let her former owner know how she's doing in her new home.

2. Write a paragraph about your favorite animal. Would it make a good pet? Explain why or why not.

3. The Pet Club does a lot of research to help them decide on a class pet. Think of an animal you don't know much about, and research it. Write a paragraph explaining some facts you learn.

TAKE A SURVEY

Sadiq and his friends took a simple survey of their class to help decide which animal they should have as a pet. Write your own pet survey. Ask your friends and family these questions to see what they think!

WHAT YOU NEED:

- a computer, phone, or tablet
- a printer
- paper

WHAT TO DO:

1. Write the questions you have for your survey on your computer, phone, tablet, or other device that can connect to a printer.

2. Leave enough space after each question so people can write down their answers.

3. Print copies of the survey to hand out to friends and family.

4. Pass the survey around to your friends and family and see what their answers are!

IDEAS FOR QUESTIONS:

- Do you have any pets?
- Do you have more than one pet?
- If you could have any pet, what kind of pet would you have?
- What kinds of pets did your parents or guardians have?
- What's your favorite animal?
- If you had to pick a class pet, which would you pick?

CREATORS

Siman Nuurali grew up in Kenya. She now lives in Minnesota. Siman and her family are Somali— just like Sadiq and his family! She and her five children love to play badminton and board games together. Siman works at Children's Hospital, and in her free time, she also enjoys writing and reading.

Anjan Sarkar is a British illustrator based in Sheffield, England. Since he was little, Anjan has always loved drawing stuff. And now he gets to draw stuff all day for his job. Hooray! In addition to the Sadiq series, Anjan has been drawing mischievous kids, undercover aliens, and majestic tigers for other exciting children's book projects.